THE IRON MAN

BY

ROBERT E. HOWARD

British Library Cataloguing-in-Publication Data
A catalogue record for this book is available from the
British Library

Contents

Robert E. Howard

Robert Ervin Howard was born in Peaster, Texas in 1906. During his youth, his family moved between a variety of Texan boomtowns, and Howard – a bookish and somewhat introverted child – was steeped in the violent myths and legends of the Old South. Although he loved reading and learning, Howard developed a distinctly Texan, hardboiled outlook on the world. He became a passionate fan of boxing, taking it up at an amateur level, and from the age of nine began to write adventure tales of semi-historical bloodshed. In 1919, when Howard was thirteen, his family moved to the Central Texas hamlet of Cross Plains, where he would stay for the rest of his life.

At fifteen Howard began to read the pulp magazines of the day, and to write more seriously. The December 1922 issue of his high school newspaper featured two of his stories, 'Golden Hope Christmas' and 'West is West'. In 1924 he sold his first piece – a short caveman tale titled 'Spear and Fang' – for $16 to the not-yet-famous *Weird Tales* magazine. He published with the magazine regularly over the next few years. 1929 was a breakout year for Howard, in that the 23-year-old writer began to sell to other magazines, such as *Ghost Stories* and *Argosy*, both of whom had previously sent him hundreds of rejection slips. In 1930, he began a correspondence with weird fiction master H. P. Lovecraft which ran up to his death six years later, and is regarded as one of the great correspondence cycles in all of fantasy literature.

It was partly due to Lovecraft's encouragement that Howard created his most famous character, Conan the Cimmerian. Conan – a barbarian-turned-King during the Hyborian Age, a mythical period of some 12,000 years ago – featured in seventeen *Weird Tales* stories between 1933 and 1936, and is now regarded as having spawned the 'sword and sorcery' genre, making Howard's influence on fantasy literature comparable to that of J. R. R. Tolkien's. The Conan stories have since been adapted many times, most famously in the series of films starring Arnold Schwarzenegger.

Howard was enjoying an all-time high in sales by the beginning of 1936, but he was also deeply upset by the ill health of his mother, who had fallen into a coma. On the morning of June 11, 1936, he asked an attending nurse whether she would ever recover, and the nurse replied negatively. Howard walked to his car, parked outside the family home in Cross Plains, and shot himself. He died eight hours later, aged just thirty.

CHAPTER I

A CANNON-BALL for a left and a thunderbolt for a right! A granite jaw, and chilled steel body! The ferocity of a tiger, and the greatest fighting heart that ever beat in an iron-ribbed breast! That was Mike Brennon, heavyweight contender.

Long before the sports writers ever heard the name of Brennon, I sat in the "athletic tent" of a carnival performing in a small Nevada town, grinning at the antics of the barker, who was volubly offering fifty dollars to anyone who could stay four rounds with "Young Firpo, the California Assassin, champeen of Los Angeles and the East Indies!" Young Firpo, a huge hairy fellow, with the bulging muscles of a weight-lifter and whose real name was doubtless Leary, stood by with a bored and contemptuous expression on his heavy features. This was an old game to him.

"Now, friends," shouted the spieler, "is they any young man here what wants to risk his life in this here ring? Remember, the management ain't responsible for life or limb! But if anybody'll git in here at his own risk-"

I saw a rough-looking fellow start up-one of the usual "plants" secretly connected with the show, of course-but at that moment the crowd set up a yell, "Brennon! Brennon! Go on, Mike!"

At last a young fellow rose from his seat, and with an embarrassed grin, vaulted over the ropes. The "plant" hesitated-Young Firpo evinced some interest, and from the hawk-like manner in which the barker eyed the newcomer, and from the roar of the crowd, I knew that he was on the "up-and-up"-a local boy, in other words.

"You a professional boxer?" asked the barker.

"I've fought some here, and in other places," answered Brennon. "But you said you barred no one."

"We don't," grunted the showman, noting the difference in the sizes of the fighters.

While the usual rigmarole of argument was gone through, I wondered how the carnival men intended saving their money if the boy happened to be too good for their man. The ring was set in the middle of the tent; the dressing-rooms were in another part. There was no curtain across the back of the ring where the local fighter could be pressed to receive a blackjack blow from the confederate behind the curtain.

Brennon, after a short trip to the dressing-room, climbed into the ring and was given a wild ovation. He was a finely built lad, six feet one in height, slim-waisted and tapering of limb, with remarkably broad shoulders and heavy arms. Dark, with narrow gray eyes, and a shock of black hair falling over a low, broad forehead, his was the true fighting face-broad across the cheekbones-with thin lips and a firm jaw. His long, smooth muscles rippled as he moved with the ease of a huge tiger. Opposed to him Young Firpo looked sluggish and ape- like.

Their weights were announced, Brennon 189, Young Firpo 191. The crowd hissed; anyone could see that the carnival boxed weighed at least 210.

THE BATTLE WAS short, fierce and sensational, and with a bedlam- like ending. At the gong Brennon sprang from his corner, coming in wide open, like a bar-room brawler. Young Firpo met him with a hard left hook to the chin, stopping him in his tracks. Brennon staggered, and the carnival boxer swung his right flush to the jaw-a terrific blow which, strangely enough, did not seem to worry Brennon as had the other. He shook his head and plunged in again, but as he did so, his foe drew back the deadly left and crashed it once more to his jaw. Brennon dropped like a log, face first. The crowd was frenzied. The barker, who was also referee, began counting swiftly, Young Firpo standing directly over the fallen warrior.

At "five!" Brennon had not twitched. At "seven!" he stirred and began making aimless motions. At "eight!" he reeled to his knees, and his reddened, dazed eyes fixed themselves on his conqueror. Instantly they blazed with the fury of the killer. As the spieler opened his mouth to say "ten!" Brennon reeled up in a blast of breath-taking ferocity that stunned the crowd.

Young Firpo, too, seemed stunned. Face whitening, he began a hurried retreat. But Brennon was after him like a blood-crazed tiger, and before the carnival fighter could lift his hands, Brennon's wide- looping left smashed under his heart and a sweeping right found his chin, crashing him face down on the canvas with a force that shook the ring.

The astounded barker mechanically began counting, but Brennon, moving like a man in a trance, pushed him away and stooping, tore the glove from Young Firpo's limp left hand. Removing something therefrom, held it up to the crowd. It was a heavy iron affair, resembling brass knuckles, and known in the parlance of the ring as a knuckle-duster. I gasped. No wonder Young Firpo had been unnerved when his victim rose! That iron-laden glove crashing twice against Brennon's jaw should have shattered the bone, yet he had been able to rise within ten seconds and finish his man with two blows!

Now all was bedlam. The barker tried to snatch the knuckle-duster from Brennon, and one of Young Firpo's seconds rushed across the ring and struck at the winner. The crowd, sensing injustice to their favorite, surged into the ring with the avowed intention of wrecking the show! As I made my way to the nearest exit I saw an infuriated townsman swing up a chair to strike the still prostrate Young Firpo. Brennon sprang forward and caught the blow on his own shoulder, going to his knees under it; then I was outside and as I walked away, laughing, I still heard the turmoil and the shouts of the policemen.

Some time later I saw Brennon fight again, in a small club on the West Coast. His opponent was a second-rater named Mulcahy. During the fight my old interest in Brennon was renewed. With incredible stamina, with as terrific a punch as I ever saw, it was evident his one failing was an absolute lack of science. Mulcahy, though strong and tough, was a mere dub, yet he clearly outboxed Brennon for nearly two rounds, and hit him with everything he had, though his best blows did not even make the dark-browed lad wince. With the second round a half minute to go, one of Brennon's sweeping swings landed and the fight was over.

I thought to myself: that lad looks like a champion, but he fights like a longshoreman, but I won't attach too much importance to that. Many a fighter stumbles through life and never learns anything, simply because of an ignorant or negligent manager.

I went to Brennon's dressing-room and spoke to him.

"My name is Steve Amber. I've seen you fight a couple of times."

"I've heard of you," he answered. "What do you want?"

Overlooking his abrupt manner, I asked: "Who's your manager?"

"I haven't any."

"How would you like me to manage you?"

"I'd as soon have you as anybody," he answered shortly. "But this was my last fight. I'm through. I'm sick of flattening dubs in fourth- rate joints."

"Tie up with me. Maybe I'll get you better matches."

"No use. I had my chance twice. Once against Sailor Slade; once against Johnny Varella. I flopped. No, don't start to argue. I don't want to talk to you-or to anybody. I'm through, and I want to go to bed."

"Suit yourself," I answered. "I never coax-but here's my card. If you change your mind, look me up."

CHAPTER II. SCENTING THE KILL.

Weeks stretched into months. But Mike Brennon was not a man one could forget easily. When I dreamed, as all fight fans and fighters' managers dream, of a super-fighter, the form of Mike Brennon rose unbidden-a dark, brooding figure, charged with the abysmal fighting fury of the primitive.

Then one day Brennon came to me-not in a day-dream, but in the flesh. He stood in the office of my training camp, his crumpled hat in his hand, an eager grin on his dark face-a very different man from the morose and moody youth to whom I had talked before.

"Mr. Amber," he said directly, "if you still want me, I'd like to have you manage me."

"That's fine," I answered.

Brennon appeared nervous.

"Can you get me a fight right away?" he asked. "I need money."

"Not so fast," I said. "I can advance you some money if you're in debt-"

He made an impatient gesture. "It's not that-can you get me a fight this week?"

"Are you in trim? How long since you've been in the ring?"

"Not since you saw me last; but I always stay in shape."

I took Brennon to my open-air ring where Spike Ganlon, a clever middleweight, was working out, and instructed them to step for a few fast rounds. Brennon was eager enough, and I was astonished to see him put up a very fair sort of boxing against the shifty Ganlon. True, he was far out-stepped and out-classed, but that was to be expected, as Ganlon was a rather prominent figure in the fistic world. But I did not like the way Mike sent in his punches. They lacked the old trip- hammer force, and he was slower than I had remembered him to be. However, when I had him slug the heavy bag he flashed his old form, nearly tearing the bag loose from its moorings, and I decided that he had been pulling his punches against Ganlon.

The days that followed were full of hard work and careful coaching. Brennon listened carefully to what Ganlon and I told him, but the result was far from satisfying. He was intelligent, but he could not seem to apply practically the things he learned easily in theory.

Still, I did not expect too much of him at first. I worked with him patiently for several weeks, importing a fairly clever heavyweight for his sparring partner. The first time they really let go, I was amazed and disappointed. Mike shuffled and floundered awkwardly with futile, flabby blows. When a sharp jab on the nose stung him, he quit trying to box and went back to his old style of wild and aimless swinging. However, these swings were the old sledge-hammer type, and his erratic speed had returned to him. I quickly called a halt.

"I'm wrong," I said. "I've been trying to make a boxing wizard out of you. But you're a natural slugger, though you seem to have little of the natural slugger's aptitude. Looks like you'd have learned something from your actual experience in the ring.

"Well, anyway, I'm going to make a real slugger like Dempsey, Sullivan and McGovern out of you. I know how you are; you've got the slugger's instinct. You can box fairly well with a friend when you're just doing it for fun, but when you're in the ring, or somebody stings you, you forget everything but your natural style. It's no discredit to a man's mentality. Dempsey was a clever boxer when he was sparring, but he never boxed in the ring. And he swung like you do, till DeForest taught him to hit straight.

"Still, Mike, I'll tell you frankly that at his crudest, Dempsey showed more aptitude for the game than you do. Now, this is for your own good. Dempsey, Ketchell and McGovern, even when they were just starting, used instinctive footwork and kept stepping around their men. They ducked and weaved and hit accurately. You go in straight up and wide open, and a blind man could duck your swings. You've unusual speed, but you don't know how to use it. But now that I know where I've been making my mistake, I'll change my tactics."

FOR A TIME it seemed as though my dreams were coming true-that Mike was a second Dempsey. In spite of his urging that I get him a fight, I kept him idle for three months-that is, he was not fighting. For hours each day I had him practice hooking the heavy bag with short smashes to straighten his punches and eliminate so much aimless swinging. He would never learn to put force behind a straight punch, but I intended making him a vicious hooker like Dempsey. And I tried to teach him the weave of that old master and the trick of boring in, protected by a barricade of gloves and elbows until in close; and the fundamentals of footwork and feinting. It was not easy.

"Mike," said Ganlon to me, "is a queer nut. He's got a fighter's heart and body, but he ain't got a fighter's brain. He understands, but he can't do what you teach him. He has to work for hours on the simplest trick-and then he's liable to forget it. If he was a bonehead, I'd understand it. But he's brainy in other ways."

"Maybe he fought so long in second-rate clubs he formed habits he can't break."

"Partly. But it goes deeper. They's a kink in his brain."

"What do you mean, a kink?" I asked uneasily.

"I dunno. But it's somethin' that breaks down his coordination and keeps his mind from workin' with his muscles. When he tries to box he has to stop and think, and in the ring you ain't got time. You see a punch comin' and in that split-second you got to know what you can't do and what you can do to get outa the way and counter. 'Course, you don't exactly study it all out, but you know, see? That is, if you're a fast boxer. If you're a wide-open slugger like Mike, you don't think nothin'. You just take the punch as a matter of course, spit out your teeth and keep borin' in."

"But any slugger is that way," I objected. "And we're not trying to teach Mike to be clever, in the technical sense of the word."

Ganlon shook his head. "I know. But Mike's different. He ain't cut out for this game. Even these simple tricks are too complicated for him. Well, he's got to learn some defense, or he'll be punched cuckoo in a few years. All the great sluggers had some. Some weaved and crouched, like Dempsey; some wrapped their arms around their skull and barged in, like Nelson and Paolino. Them that fought wide open didn't last no time, 'specially among the heavies. The padded cell and paper- doll cut-outs for most of 'em. It don't stand to reason a human skull can stand up under the beatin's it gets like that."

"You're a born croaker. Mike's rugged but intelligent. He'll learn."

"At anything else, yes-at this game-maybe."

NOT LONG AFTER my talk with Spike, Brennon came to me.

"Steve," he said, "I've got to have a fight. I need money-bad."

"Mike," said I, "it's none of my business, but I don't see why you should be so desperately insistent. You've been at no expense at all, here in the camp. You said you weren't in debt, and you've refused my offer to loan you-"

"What business is it of yours?" he broke in, white at the lips.

"None at all," I hastened to assure him. "Only as your manager, I've got your financial interests at heart, naturally. I apologize."

"I apologize, too, Steve," he answered abruptly, his manner changing. "I should have known you weren't trying to pry into my private affairs. But I've got to have at least-" And he named a sum of money which rather surprised me.

"There's only one way to get that much," I answered. "Understand, I don't believe you're ready to go in with a first-string man. But since money is the object-Monk Barota is on the coast now, padding his kayo record. He'll be looking for set-ups. The promoter at the Hopi A.C. is a friend of mine. I can get you a match with him at close to the figure you named. You understand that a bad defeat now might ruin you. Don't say I didn't warn you. But you're in fine

14

shape, and if you fight as we've taught you, I believe you can whip him."

"I'll whip him," Mike nodded grimly.

I hoped he was more sincere in his belief than I was. I really felt in my heart that he was not ready for a first-rater and I had intended building him up more gradually. But there was fierce, driving intensity about him when he spoke of the money he needed that broke down my resolution. Brennon was, in many ways, a character of terrific magnetic force. Like Sullivan, he dominated all about him, trainers, handlers and matchmakers. But only in the matter of money was he unreasonable, and this quirk in his nature amounted to an obsession.

Mainly through my influence, Brennon, an entirely unknown quantity, was matched with Barota for a ten-rounder; at ringside the odds were three to one on the Italian, with no takers. My last instructions to Mike were: "Remember! Use the crouch and guard Ganlon taught you. If you don't have some defense, he'll ruin you!"

The lights went out except those over the ring. The gong sounded. The crowd fell silent-that breathless, momentary silence that marks the beginning of the fight. The men slid out of their corners and-

"Oh, my gosh!" wailed Ganlon at my side. "He's doin' everything backward!"

Mike wore his old uncertain manner. Under the lights, with his foe before him and the roar of the crowd deafening him, he was like a trapped jungle beast, bewildered and confused. Barota led-Mike ducked clumsily the wrong way, and took the punch in the eye. That flicking left was hard for any man to avoid, but Mike incessantly ducked into it.

Ganlon was raving at my side. "After all these months of work, he forgets! You better throw in the sponge now. Look there!" as Mike tried a left of his own. "He can't even hook right. The whole house knows what's comin'. Same as writin' a letter about it."

BAROTA WAS TAKING his time. In spite of the fact that his foe seemed to have nothing but a scowl, no man could look into Mike Brennon's face and take him lightly. But a round of clumsy floundering and ineffectual pawing lulled his suspicions. Meanwhile, he flitted around the bewildered slugger, showering him with stinging left jabs. Ganlon was nearly weeping with rage as if his pupil's inaptness somehow reflected on him.

"All I know, I taught him, and there's that wop makin' a monkey outa him!"

With the round thirty seconds to go, Barota suddenly tore in with one of his famous attacks. Mike abandoned all attempts at science and began swinging wildly and futilely. Barota worked untouched between his flailing arms, beating a rattling barrage against Brennon's head and body. The gong stopped the punishment.

Mike's face was somewhat cut, but he was as fresh as if he had not just gone through a severe beating. He broke in on Ganlon's impassioned soliloquy to remark: "This fellow can't hit."

"Can't hit!" Ganlon nearly dropped the sponge. "Why, he's got a kayo record as long as a subway! Ain't he just pounded you all over the ring?"

"I didn't feel his punches, anyway," answered Mike, and then the gong sounded.

Barota came out fast, in a mood to bring this fight to a sudden close. He launched a swift attack, cut Mike's lips with a right; then began hammering at his body with the left-handed assault which had softened so many of his opponents for the kayo. The crowd went wild as he battered Mike around the ring, but suddenly I felt Ganlon's fingers sink into my arm.

"Bat Nelson true to life!" he whispered, his voice vibrating with excitement. "The crowd thinks, and Barota thinks, them left hooks is hurtin' Mike-but he ain't even feelin' 'em. He's got one chance-when Barota shoots the right-"

At this moment Barota stepped back, feinted swiftly and shot the right. He was proud of the bone-crushing quality of that right hand. He had a clear opening and every ounce of his weight went behind it. The leather-guarded knuckles backed by spar-like arm and heavy shoulder, crashed flush against Mike's jaw. The impact was plainly heard in every part of the house. A gasp went up, nails sank deep into clenching palms. Mike swayed drunkenly, but he did not fall.

Barota stopped short for a flashing instant-frozen by the realization that he had failed to even floor his man. And in that second Mike swung a wild left and landed for the first time-high on the cheek bone, but Barota went down. The crowd rose screaming. Dazed, the Italian rose without a count and Mike tore into him with the ferocity of a tiger that scents the kill. Barota, blinded and dizzy, was in no condition to defend himself, yet Mike missed with both hands until a mine-sweeping right-hander caught his man flush on the temple, and he dropped-not merely out, but senseless.

The crowd was in a frenzy, but Ganlon said to me: "He's an iron man, don't you see? A natural-born freak like Grim and Goddard. He'll never learn anything, not if he trains a hundred years."

CHAPTER III. WHITE HOT FIGHTING FURY.

THE DAY AFTER Mike Brennon had shocked the sporting world by his victory, he, Ganlon and I sat at breakfast, and we were a far from merry gang. Ganlon read the morning papers and growled.

"The whole country's on fire," he muttered. "Sports writers goin' cuckoo over the new find. Tellin' Barota cried and took on in his dressin'-room when he come to; and talkin' about how Mike 'fooled' his man in the first round by lookin' like a dub-callin' him a second Fitzsimmons! Applesauce. But here's a old-timer that knows his stuff.

"'If I am not much mistaken,'" he read, "'this Brennon is the same who looked like a deckhand against Sailor Slade in Los Angeles last year. His kayo of Barota had all the earmarks of a fluke. He is, however, incredibly tough.'

"Uhmhuh," said Ganlon, laying down the paper. "Quite true. Mike, I hate to say it, but as a fighter you're a false alarm. It ain't your fault. You got the heart and the body, but you got no more natural talent than a ribbon clerk, and you can't learn. You got the fightin' instinct, but not the fighter's instinct-and they's a flock of difference.

"You're just a heavyweight Joe Grim. A iron man; never was one but Jeffries who could learn anything. I'm advisin' you to quit the ring- now. Your kind don't come to no good end. Too many punches on the head. They get permanently punch drunk. You don't have to go around countin' your fingers; you got brains enough to succeed somewhere else.

"You got three courses to follow: first, you can go around fightin' set-ups at the small clubs. You can make a livin' that way, and last a long time. Second, you can sign up with some of the offers you're bound to get now. Fightin' clever first-raters you won't win much, if any, but you'll be an attraction like Grim was. But you won't last. You'll crack under the incessant fire of smashes, and wind up in the booby hatch. Third and best, you can take what money you got and step out. Me and Steve will gladly lend you enough to start in business in a modest way."

I nodded. Mike shook his head and spread his iron fingers on the table in front of him. As usual he dominated the scene-a great somber figure of unknown potentialities.

"You're right, Spike, in everything you've said. I've always known there was a deficiency somewhere. No man could be as impervious to punishment as I am and have a perfectly normal brain. Not alone at boxing; I've failed at everything else I've tried. As for boxing, the crowd dazes me, for one thing. But that isn't all. I just can't remember what to do next, and have to struggle through the best way I can.

"But-I can take it! That's my one hope. That's why I'm not quitting the game. At the cost of my reflexes, maybe,

Nature gave me an unusual constitution. You admit I'd be a drawing card. Well, I'm like Battling Nelson-not human when it comes to taking punishment. The only man that ever hurt me was Sailor Slade, and he couldn't stop me. Nobody can now. Eventually, after years of battering, someone will knock me out. But before that time, I'm going to cash in on my ruggedness. Capitalize on the fact that no man can keep me down for the count. I'll accumulate a fortune if I'm handled right."

"Great heavens, man!" I exclaimed. "Do you realize what that means-the frightful punishment, the mutilations? You'll be fighting first-raters now-men with skill and terrific punches. You have no defense. You sap, they'd hammer you to a red pulp."

"My defense is a granite jaw and iron ribs," he answered. "I'll take them all on and wear them down."

"Maybe," I answered. "A man can wear himself down punching a granite boulder, as I've seen men do with Tom Sharkey and Joe Goddard, but what about the boulder! You were lucky with Barota. The next man will watch his step."

"They can't hurt me. And I can beat any man I can hit. Win or lose, I'll be a drawing card, and that means big purses. That's what I'm after. Do you think I'd go through this purgatory if the need wasn't great?"

"If it's poverty-" I began.

"What do you know about poverty?" he cried in a strange passion. "Were you left in a basket on the steps of an orphanage almost as soon as you were born? Did you spend your childhood mixed in with five hundred others, where the needs of all were so great that no one of you got more than the barest necessities? Did you pass your boyhood as a tramp and hobo worker, riding the rods and starving? I did!

"But that's neither here nor there; nor it isn't my own personal poverty so much that drove me back in the ring-but let it pass. As my manager, I want you to get busy. If I can win another fight it will increase my prestige. I don't expect to win many. Later on, they'll come packing in to see me, for the same reason they went to see Joe Grim-to see if I can be knocked out. Until the fans find out I'm a freak, I'll have to go on my merits. Barota wants a return match. I don't want him now, or any other clever man who'll outpoint me and make me look even worse than I am. I want the fans to see me bloody and staggering-and still carrying on! That's what draws the crowd. Get me a mankiller-a puncher who'll come in and try to murder me. Get me Jack Maloney!"

"It's suicide!" I cried. "Maloney'll kill you! I won't have anything to do with it!"

"Then, by heaven," Brennon roared, heaving erect and crashing his fist on the table, "our ways part here! You could help me better than anyone else-you know the ballyhoo. But if you fail me-"

"If you're determined," I said huskily, my mind almost numbed by the driving force of his will-power, "I'll do all I can. But I warn you, you'll leave this game with a clouded brain."

His nervous grip nearly crushed my fingers as he said shortly: "I knew you'd stand by me. Never mind my brain; it's cased in solid iron."

As he strode out Ganlon, slightly pale, said to me in a low voice: "A twist in his head sure. Money-all the time-money. I'm no dude, but he dresses like a wharfhand. What's he do with his money? He ain't supportin' no aged mother, it's a cinch. You heard him say he was left on a doorstep."

I shook my head. Brennon was an enigma beyond my comprehension.

THE RISE OF Iron Mike Brennon is now ring history, and of all the vivid pages in the annals of this heart-stirring game, I hold that the story of this greatest of all iron men makes the most lurid, fantastic and pulse-quickening chapter.

Iron Mike Brennon! Look at him as he was when his exploits swept the country. Six feet one from his narrow feet to the black tousled shock of his hair; one hundred and ninety pounds of steel springs and whalebone. With his terrible eyes glaring from under heavy black brows, thin, blood-smeared lips writhed in snarl of battle fury-still when I dream of the super-fighter there rises the picture of Mike

Brennon-a dream charged with bitterness. Take a man with incredible stamina and hitting power; take from him the ability to remember one iota of science in actual combat and leave out of his make-up the instinct of the natural fighter, and you have Iron Mike Brennon. A man who would have been the greatest champion of all time, but for that flaw in his make-up.

His first fight, after that memorable breakfast table conversation, was with Jack Maloney-one hundred and ninety-five pounds of white-hot fighting fury, with a right hand like a caulking mallet. They met at San Francisco.

With the aid of Ganlon and friendly scribes, I set the old ballyhoo working. The papers were full of Mike Brennon. They pointed out that he had over twenty knockouts to his credit, ignoring the fact that all of these victims, except one, were unknown dubs. They glossed over the fact that he had been out-pointed by second-raters and beaten to a pulp by Sailor Slade. They angrily refuted charges that his kayo of Barota was a fluke.

The stadium was packed that night. The crowd paid their money, and they got its worth. Before the bell I was whispering a few instructions which I knew would be useless, when Mike cut in with fierce eagerness: "What a sell-out! Look at that crowd! If I win it'll mean more sell-outs and bigger purses! I've got to win!" His eyes gleamed with ferocious avidity.

Two giants crashed from their corners as the gong sounded. Maloney came in like the great slugger he was, body crouched, chin tucked behind his shoulder, hands high. Brennon, forgetting everything before the blast of the crowd and his own fighting fury, rushed like a longshoreman, head lifted, hands clenched at his hips, wide open-as iron men have fought since time immemorial-with but one thought-to get to his foe and crush him.

Maloney landed first, a terrific left hook which spattered Brennon with blood and brought the crowd to its feet, roaring. I heard a note of relief in the shouts of Maloney's manager. This bird was going to be easy, after all! Like most sluggers, when they find a man they can hit easily, Maloney had gone fighting crazy. He lashed Brennon about the ring, hitting so hard and fast that Mike had no time to get set. The few swings he did try swished harmlessly over Maloney's bobbing head.

"He's slowin' down," muttered Ganlon as the first round drew to a close. "The old iron man game! Maloney's punchin' hisself out."

True, Jack's blows were coming not weaker, but slower. No man could keep up the pace he was setting. Brennon was as strong as ever, and just before the gong he staggered Maloney with a sweeping left to the body-his first blow.

Back in his corner Ganlon wiped the blood from Mike's battered face and grinned savagely: "Joe Goddard had nothin' on you. I'm beginnin' to believe you'll beat him. You've took plenty and you'll take more; he'll come out strong but each round he'll get weaker; he'll be fought out."

THE FANS THUNDERED acclaim as Maloney rushed out for the second. But he had sensed something they had not. He had hit this man with everything he possessed and had failed to even floor him. So he tore in like a wild man, and again drove Brennon about the ring before a torrent of left and right hooks that sounded like the kicks of a mule. Brennon, eyes nearly closed, lips pulped, nose broken, showed no sign of distress until the latter part of the round, when Maloney landed repeatedly to the jaw with his maul-like right. Then Mike's knees trembled momentarily, but he straightened and cut his foe's cheek with a glancing right.

At the gong the crowd began to realize what was going on. The timbre of their yells changed. They began to inquire at the top of their voices if Maloney was losing his famed punch, or if Brennon was made of solid iron.

Ganlon, wiping Brennon's gory features and offering the smelling salts, which he pushed away, said swiftly: "Maloney's legs trembled as he went back to his corner; he looked back over his shoulder like he couldn't believe it when he saw you walk to your corner without a quiver. He knows he ain't lost his punch! He knows you're the first man ever stood up to him wide open; he knows you been through a tough grind and ain't even saggin'. You got his goat. Now go get him!"

The gong sounded. Maloney came in, the light of desperation in his eyes, to redeem his slipping fame as a knocker-out. His blows were like a rain of sledge-hammers and before that rain Mike Brennon went down. The referee began counting. Maloney reeled back against the ropes, breath coming in great gasps-completely fought out.

"He'll get up," said Ganlon calmly.

Brennon was half crouching on his knees, dazed, not hurt. I saw his lips move and I read their motion: "More fights-more money-"

He bounded erect. Maloney's whole body sagged. Brennon's rising took more morale out of Jack than any sort of a blow would have done. Mike, sensing the mental condition and physical weariness of Maloney, tore in like a tiger. Left, right, he missed, shaking off Maloney's weakening blows as if they had been slaps from a girl. At last he landed-a wide left hook to the head. Maloney tottered, and a wild over-hand right crashed under his cheek bone, dashing him to his knees. At "nine!" he staggered up, but another right that a blind man in good condition could have ducked, dropped him again. The referee hesitated, then raised Mike's hand, beckoning to Maloney's seconds.

As Maloney, aided by his handlers, reeled to his corner on buckling legs, I noted the ironical fact: the winner was a gory, battered wreck, while the loser had only a single cut on his cheek. I thought of the old fights in which iron men of another day had figured: of Joe Goddard, the old Barrier Champion, outlasting the great Choynski, finishing each of their terrible battles a bloody travesty of a man, but winner. I thought of Sharkey dropping Kid McCoy; of Nelson outlasting Gans; Young Corbett-Herrerra. And I sighed. Of all the men who relied on their ruggedness to carry them through, Brennon was the most wide open, the most erratic.

As I sponged his cuts in the dressing-room, I could not help saying: "You see what fighting a first-string hitter means; you won't be able to answer the gong for months."

"Months!" he mumbled through smashed lips. "You'll sign me up with Johnny Varella for a bout next week!"

CHAPTER IV. IRON MIKE'S DREAD.

AFTER THE MALONEY fight, fans and scribes realized what he was-an iron man-and as such his fame grew. He became a drawing card just as he had predicted-one of the greatest of his day. And his inordinate lust for money grew with his power as an attraction. He haggled over prices, held out for every cent he could get, and rather than pass up a fight, would always lower his price. For the first and only time in my life, I was merely a figure-head. Brennon was the real power behind the curtain. And he insisted on fighting at least once a month.

"You'll crack three times as quickly fighting so often," I protested. "Otherwise you might last for years."

"But why stretch it out if I can make the same amount of money in a few months that I could make in that many years?"

"But consider the strain on you!" I cried.

"I'm not considering anything about myself," he answered roughly. "Get me a match."

The matches came readily. He had caught the crowd's fancy and no matter whom he fought, the fans flocked to see him. He met them all- ferocious sluggers, clever dancers, and dangerous fighters who combined the qualities of slugger and boxer. When first-rate opponents were not forthcoming quickly enough, he went into the sticks and pushed over second-raters. As long as he was making money, no matter how much or how little, he was satisfied. What he did with that money, I did not know. He was honest, always shot square with his obligations; but beyond that he was a miser. He lived at the training camps or at the cheapest hotels, in spite of my protests; he bought cheap clothes and allowed himself no luxuries whatever.

At first he won consistently. He was dangerous to any man. Coupled with his abnormal endurance was a mental state-a driving, savage determination-which dragged him off the canvas time and again. This was above and beyond his natural fighting fury, and he had acquired it between the time he had first retired and the next time I saw him.

At the time he was in his prime, there was a wealth of material in the heavyweight ranks, and Brennon loomed among them as the one man none of them could stop. That fact alone put him on equal footing with men in every other way his superiors.

Following the Maloney fight, the public clamored for a match between my iron man and Yon Van Heeren, the Durable Dutchman, who was considered, up to that time, the toughest man in the world, one who had never been knocked out, and whose only claim to fame, like Brennon's, was his ruggedness. A certain famous scribe, referring to this fight as "a brawl between two bar-room thugs," said: "This unfortunate affair has set the game back twenty years. No sensitive person seeing this slaughter for his or her first fight, could ever be tempted to see another. People who do not know the game are likely to judge it by the two gorillas, who, utterly devoid of science, turned the ring into a shambles."

Before the men went into the ring they made the referee promise not to stop the fight under any circumstances-an unusual proceeding, but easily understood in their case.

THE FIGHT WAS a strange experience to Mike; most of the punishment was on the other side. Van Heeren, six feet two and weighing 210 pounds, was a terrific hitter, but lacked Mike's dynamic speed and fury. Those sweeping haymakers which had missed so many others, crashed blindingly against the Dutchman's head or sank agonizingly into his body. At the end of the first round his face was a gory wreck. At the end of the fourth his features had lost all human semblance; his body was a mass of reddened flesh.

Toe to toe they stood, round after round, neither taking a back step. The fifth, sixth and seventh rounds were nightmares, in which Mike was dropped three times, and Van Heeren went down twice that many times. All over the stadium women were fainting or being helped out; fans were shrieking for the fight to be stopped.

In the ninth, Van Heeren, a hideous and inhuman sight, dropped for the last time. Four ribs broken, features permanently ruined, he lay writhing, still trying to rise as the referee tolled off the "Ten!" that marked his finish as a fighting man.

Mike Brennon, clinging to the ropes, dizzy and nearly punched out for the only time in his life, stood above his victim, acknowledged king of all iron men. This fight finished Van Heeren, and nearly finished boxing in the state, but it added to Brennon's fame, and his real pity for the broken Dutchman was mingled with a fierce exultation of realized power. More money-more packed houses! The world's greatest iron man! In the three years he fought under my management he met them all, except the champion of his division. He lost about as many as he won, but the only thing that could impair his drawing power was a knockout-and this seemed postponed indefinitely. He won more of his fights against the hard punchers than against the light tappers, as the latter took no chances. Many a slugger, after battering him to a red ruin, blew up and fell before his aimless but merciless attack. He broke the hands and he broke the hearts of the men who tried to stop him.

The light hitters outboxed him, but did not hurt him, and his wild swings were dangerous even to them. Barota outpointed him, and Jackie Finnegan, Frankie Grogan and Flash Sullivan, the lightheavy champion.

The hard hitters made the mistake of trading punches with him. Soldier Handler dropped him five times in four rounds, and then stopped a right-hander that knocked him clear out of the ring and into fistic oblivion. Jose Gonzales, the great South American, punched himself out on the iron tiger and went down to defeat. Gunboat Sloan battered out a red decision over him, but still believing he could achieve the impossible, went in to trade punches in a return bout, and lasted less than a round. Brennon finished Ricardo Diaz, the Spanish Giant, and beat down Snake Calberson after his toughness had broken the Brown Phantom's heart. Johnny Varella and several lesser lights broke their hands on him and quit. He met Whitey Broad and Kid Allison in no decision bouts; knocked out Young Hansen, and fought a fierce fifteen-round draw with Sailor Steve Costigan, who never rated better than a second-class man, but who gave some first-raters terrific battles.

To those who doubt that flesh and blood can endure the punishment which Brennon endured, I beg you to look at the records of the ring's iron men. I point to your attention, Tom Sharkey plunging headlong into the terrible blows of Jeffries; that same Sharkey shooting headlong over the ropes onto the concrete floor from the blows of Choynski, yet finishing the fight a winner.

I call to your attention Mike Boden, who had no more defense than had Brennon, staying the limit with Choynski; and Joe Grim taking all Fitzsimmons could hand him-was it fifteen or sixteen times he was floored? Yet he finished that fight standing. No man can understand the iron men of the ring. Theirs is a long, hard, bloody trail, with oftentimes only poverty and a clouded mind at the end, but the red chapter their clan has written across the chronicles of the game will never be effaced.

And so Brennon fought on, taking all his cruel punishment, hoarding his money, saying little-as much a mystery to me as ever. Sports writers discovered his passion for money, and raked him. They accused him of being miserly and refusing aid to his less fortunate fellows-the battered tramps who will occasionally touch a successful fighter for a hand-out. This was only partly true. He did sometimes give money to men who needed it desperately, but the occasions were infrequent.

Then he began to crack. Ganlon, his continual champion, first sensed it. Crouching beside me the night Mike fought Kid Allison, Spike whispered to me out of the corner of his mouth: "He's slowin' down. It's the beginnin' of the end."

THAT NIGHT SPIKE spoke plainly to his friend.

"Mike, you're about through. You're slippin'. Punches jar you worse than they used to. You've lasted three years of terrible hard goin'. You got to quit."

"When I'm knocked out," said Mike stubbornly. "I haven't taken the count yet."

"When a bird like you takes the count, it means he's a punch-drunk wreck," said Ganlon. "When the blows begin to hurt you, it means the shock of them is reachin' the brain and hurtin' it. Remember Van Heeren, that you finished? He's wanderin' around, sayin' he's trainin' to fight Fitzsimmons, that's been dead for years."

A shadow crossed Mike's dark face at the mention of the Dutchman's name. The beatings he had taken had disfigured him and given him a peculiarly sinister look, which however, did not rob his face of its strange dominating quality.

"I'm good for a few more fights," he answered. "I need money-"

"Always money!" I exclaimed. "You must have half a million dollars at least. I'm beginning to believe you are a miser-"

"Steve," said Ganlon suddenly, "Van Heeren was around here yesterday."

"What of it?"

Ganlon continued almost accusingly, "Mike gave him a thousand dollars."

"What if I did?" cried Brennon in one of his rare inexplicable passions. "The fellow was broke-in no condition to earn any money-I finished him-why shouldn't I help him a little? Whose business is it?"

"Nobody's," I answered. "But it shows you're not a miser. And it deepens the mystery about you. Won't you tell me why you need more money?"

He made a quick impatient gesture. "There's no need. You get the matches-I do the fighting. We split the money, and that's all there is to it."

"But, Mike," I said as kindly as I could, "there is more to it. You've made me more money than either of the champions I've managed, and if I didn't sincerely wish for your own good, I'd say for you to stay in the ring.

"But you ought to quit. You can even get your features fixed up-plastic face building is a wonderful art. Fight even one more time, and you may spend your days in a padded cell."

"I'm tougher than you think," he answered. "I'm as good as I ever was and I'll prove it. Get me Sailor Slade."

"He beat you once before, when you were better than you are now. How do you expect-"

"I didn't have the incentive to win then, that I have now."

I nodded. What this incentive was I did not know, but I had seen him rise again and again from what looked like certain defeat-had seen him, writhing on the canvas, turn white, his eyes blue with sudden terror as he dragged himself upright. Terror? Of losing! A terror that kept him going when even his iron body was tottering on the verge of collapse and when the old fighting frenzy had ceased to function in the numbed brain. What prompted this dread?

It was a mystery I could not fathom, but that in some way it was connected with his strange money-lust, I knew.

"You'll sign me for four fights," Brennon was saying. "With Sailor Slade, Young Hansen, Jack Slattery and Mike Costigan."

"You're out of your head!" I exclaimed sharply. "You've picked the four most dangerous battlers in the world!"

"Hansen, it'll be easy. I beat him once, and I can do it again. I don't know about Slattery. I want to take him on last. First, I've got to hurdle Slade. After him, I'll fight Costigan. He's the least scientific of the four, but the hardest hitter. If I'm slipping I want to get him before I've gone too far."

"It's suicide!" I cried. "If you've got to fight, pass up these mankillers and take on some set-ups. If Slade don't knock you out, he'll soften you up so Costigan will punch you right into the bughouse. He's a murderer. They call him Iron Mike, too."

"I'll pack them in," he answered heedlessly. "Slade's nearly the drawing card I am, and as for Costigan, the fans always turn out to see two iron men meet."

As usual, there was no answer to be made.

CHAPTER V. THE ROLL OF THE IRON MEN.

IT WAS A few nights before the Brennon-Slade fight. I had wandered into Mike's room and my eye fell on a partially completed letter on his writing table. Without any intention of spying, I idly noted that it was addressed to a girl named Marjory Walshire, at a very fashionable girls' school in New York state.

I saw that a letter from this girl lay beside the other one, and though it was an atrocious breach of manners, in my curiosity to know why a girl in a society school like that would be writing a prize- fighter, I picked up the partially completed letter and glanced idly over it. The next moment I was reading it with fierce intensity, all scruples, forgotten. Having finished it, I snatched up the other and ruthlessly tore it open.

I had scarcely finished reading this when Mike entered with Ganlon. His eyes blazed with sudden fury, but before he could say a word I launched an offensive of my own-for one of the few times in my life, wild with rage.

"You born fool!" I snarled. "So this is why you've been crucifying yourself!"

"What do you mean by getting into my private correspondence?" his voice was husky with fury.

I sneered. "I'm not going to enter into a discussion of etiquette. You can beat me up afterward, but just now I'm going to have my say.

"You've been keeping some girl in a ritzy finishing school back East. Finishing school! It's nearly finished you! What kind of a girl is she, to let you go through this mill for her? I'd like for her to see your battered map now! While she's been lolling at ease in the most expensive school she could find, you've been flattening out the resin with your shoulders and soaking it down with your blood-"

"Shut up!" roared Brennon, white and shaking.

He leaned back against the table, gripping the edge so hard his knuckles whitened as he fought for control. At last he spoke more calmly.

"Yes, that's the incentive that's kept me going. That girl is the only girl I ever loved-the only thing I ever had to love.

"Listen, do you know how lonely a kid is when he has absolutely nobody in the world to love? The folks in the home were kind, but there were so many children-I got the beginnings of a good education. That's all.

"Out in the world it was worse. I worked, tramped, starved. I fought for everything I ever got. I have a better education than most, you say. I worked my way through high school, and read all the books in my spare time that I could beg, steal or borrow. Many a time I went hungry to buy a book.

"I drifted into the ring from fighting in carnivals and the like. I never got anywhere. After I whipped Mulcahy the night you talked to me, I quit. Drifted. Then in a little town on the Arizona desert I met Marjory Walshire.

"Poverty? She knew poverty! Working her fingers to the bone in a cafe. Good blood in her too, just as there is in me, somewhere. She should have been born to the satins and velvets-instead she was born to the greasy dishes and dirty tables of a second-class cafe. I loved her, and she loved me. She told me her dreams that she never believed would come true-of education-nice clothes-refined companions-every thing that any girl wants.

"Where was I to turn? I could take her out of the cafe-only to introduce her to the drudgery of a laboring man's wife. So I went back into the ring. As soon as I could, I sent her to school. I've been sending her money enough to live as well as any girl there, and I've saved too, so when she gets out of school and I have to quit the ring, we can be married and start in business that won't mean drudgery and poverty.

"Poverty is the cause of more crimes, cruelty and suffering than anything else. Poverty kept me from having a home and people like other kids. You know how it is in the slums-parents toiling for a living and too many children. They can't support them all. Mine left me on the door-step of the orphanage with a note: 'He's honest born. We love him, but we can't keep him. Call him Michael Brennon.'

"Poverty can be as cruel in a small town as in a city-Marjory, who'd never been out of the town where she was born-with her soul starved and her little white hands reddened and callused-

"It's the thought of her that's kept me on my feet when the whole world was blind and red and the fists of my opponent were like hammers on my shattering brain-that's the thought that dragged me off the canvas when my body was without feeling and my arms hung like lead, to strike down the man I could no longer see. And as long as she's waiting for me at the end of the long trail, there's no man on earth can make me take the count!"

His voice crashed through the room like a clarion call of victory, but my old doubts returned.

"But how can she love you so much," I exclaimed, "when she's willing for you to go through all this for her?"

"What does she know of fighting? I made her believe boxing was more or less of a dancing and tapping affair. She'd heard of Corbett and Tunney, clever fellows who could step twenty rounds without a mark, and she supposed I was like them. She hasn't seen me in nearly four years-not since I left the town where she worked. I've put her off when she's wanted to come and see me, or for me to come to her. When she does see my battered face it'll be a terrible shock to her, but I was never very handsome anyway-"

"Do you mean to tell me," I broke in, "that she never tunes in on one of your fights, never reads an account of them, when the papers are full of your doings?"

"She don't know my real name. After I quit the game the first time, I went under the name of Mike Flynn to duck the two-by-four promoters I'd fought for, and who were always pestering me to fight for them again. The first time I saw Marjory I began to think of fighting again, and I never told her differently. The money I've sent has been in cashier's checks. To her, I'm simply Mike Flynn, a fighter she never hears of. She wouldn't recognize my picture in the papers."

"But her letters are addressed to Mike Brennon."

"You didn't look closely. They're addressed to Michael Flynn, care of Mike Brennon, this camp. She thinks Brennon is merely a friend of her Mike. Well, now you know why I've fought on and stinted myself. With Van Heeren, it was different. I'm responsible for his condition. I had to help him.

"These four fights now; one of them may be my last. I've got money, but I want more. I intend that Marjory shall never want again for anything. I'm to get a hundred grand for this fight. My third purse of that size. With good management, thanks to you, I've made more money than many champions. If I whip these four men, I'll fight on. If I'm knocked out, I'll have to quit. Let's drop the matter."

I HAVEN'T THE heart to tell of the Brennon-Slade fight in detail. Even today the thought of the punishment Mike took that night takes the stiffening out of my knees. He had slipped even more than we had thought. The steel-spring legs, which had carried him through so many whirlwind battles, had slowed down. His sweeping haymakers crashed over with their old power, but they did not continually wing through the air as of old. Blows that should not have jarred him, staggered him. The squat sailor, wild with the thought of a knockout, threw caution to the winds. How many times he floored Mike I never dared try to remember, but Brennon was still Iron Mike. Again and again the gong saved him; in the fourteenth round Slade went to pieces, and the iron tiger he had punched into a red smear, found him in the crimson mist and blindly blasted him into unconsciousness.

Brennon collapsed in his corner after Slade was counted out, and both men were carried senseless from the ring. I sat by Mike's side that night while he lay in a semi-conscious state, occasionally muttering brokenly as his bruised brain conjured up red visions. He lay, both eyes closed, his oft-broken nose a crushed ruin, cut and gashed all about the head and face, now and then stirring uneasily as the pain of three broken ribs stabbed him.

For the first time he spoke the name of the girl he loved, groping out his hands like a lost child. Again he fought over his fearful battles and his mighty fists clenched until the knuckles showed white and low bestial snarls tore through his battered lips.

In his delirium he raised himself painfully on one elbow, his burning, unseeing eyes gleaming like slits of flame between the battered lids; he spoke in a low voice as if answering and listening to the murmur of ghosts: "Joe Grim! Battling Nelson! Mike Boden! Joe Goddard! Iron Mike Brennon!"

My flesh crawled. I cannot impart to you the uncanniness of hearing the roll call of those iron men of days gone by, muttered in the stillness of night through the pulped and delirious lips of the grimmest of them all.

At last he fell silent, and went into a natural slumber. As I went softly into the other room, Ganlon entered, his savage eyes blazing with fierce triumph. With him was a girl-a darling of high society she seemed, with her costly garments and air of culture, but she exhibited an elemental anxiety such as no pampered and sophisticated debutante would, or could have done.

"Where is he?" she cried desperately. "Where is Mike? I must see him!"

"He's asleep now," I said shortly, and added in my cruel bitterness: "You've done enough to him already. He wouldn't want you to see him like he is now."

She cringed as from a blow. "Oh, let me just look in from the door," she begged, twining her white hands together-and I thought of how often Mike's hands had been bathed in blood for her-"I won't wake him."

I hesitated and her eyes flamed; now she was the primal woman.

"Try to stop me and I'll kill you!" she cried, and rushed past me into the room.

CHAPTER VI. A CINCH TO WIN!

THE GIRL STOPPED short on the threshold. Mike muttered restlessly in his sleep and turned his blind eyes toward the door, but did not waken. As the girl's eyes fell on that frightfully disfigured face, she swayed drunkenly; her hands went to her temples and a low whimper like an animal in pain escaped her. Then, her face corpse-white and her eyes set in a deathly stare, she stole to the bedside and with a heart-rending sob, sank to her knees, cradling that battered head in her arms.

Mike muttered, but still he did not waken. At last I drew her gently away and led her into the next room, closing the door behind us. There she burst into a torrent of weeping. "I didn't know!" she kept sobbing over and over. "I didn't know fighting was like that! He told me never to go to a fight, or listen to one over the radio, and I obeyed him. Why, how could I know-here's one of the few letters in which he even mentioned his fights. I've kept them all."

The date was over three years old. I read: "Last night I stopped Jack Maloney, a foremost contender. He scarcely laid a glove on me. Don't worry about me, darling, this game is a cinch."

I laughed bitterly, remembering the gory wreck Maloney had made of Mike before he went out.

"I've been doing you an injustice," I said. "I didn't think a man could keep a girl in such ignorance as to the real state of things, but it's true. You're O.K. Maybe you can persuade Mike to give up the game-we can't."

"Surely he can't be thinking of fighting again if he lives?" she cried.

I laughed. "He won't die. He'll be laid up a while, that's all. Now I'll take you to a hotel-"

"I'm going to stay here close to Mike," she answered passionately. "I could kill myself when I think how he's suffered for me. Tomorrow I'm going to marry him and take him away."

After she was settled in a spare room, I turned to Spike: "I guess you're responsible for this. You might have waited till Mike was out of bed. That was a terrible shock for her."

"I intended it should be," he snarled. "I wrote and told her did she know her boy Mike Flynn was really Mike Brennon which was swiftly bein' punched into the booby-hatch? And I gave her some graphic accounts of his battles. I wrote her in time for her to get here to see the fight, but she says she missed a train."

"Let him fight," Spike spat. "Costigan will kill him, if they fight. I've seen these iron men crack before. I was in Tom Berg's corner the night Jose Gonzales knocked him out, and he died while the referee was countin' over him. Some men you got to kill to stop. Mike Brennon's one of 'em. If the girl's got a spark of real womanhood in her, she'll persuade him to quit."

Morning found the battered iron man clear of mind, his super-human recuperative powers already asserting themselves. I brought Marjory to his bedside and before he could say anything, I left them alone. Later she came to me, her eyes red with weeping.

"I've argued and begged," she cried desperately, "but he won't give in!"

All of us surrounded Mike's bedside. "Mike," I said, "you're a fool. The punches have gone to your head. You can't mean you'll fight again!"

"I'm good for some more big purses," he replied with a grin.

Marjory cried out as if he had stabbed her. "Mike-oh, Mike! We have more money now than we'll ever use. You haven't been fair to me. I'd have rather gone in rags, and worked my fingers to the bone in the lowest kind of drudgery than to have you suffer!"

His face lighted with a rare smile. He reached out a hand, amazingly gentle, and took one of the girl's soft hands in his own.

"White little hands," he murmured. "Soft, as they were meant to be, now. Why, just looking at you repays me a thousand times for all I've gone through. And what have I gone through? A few beatings. The old-timers took worse, and got little or nothing."

"But there's no reason for your crucifying yourself-and me-any longer."

He shook his head with that strange abnormal stubbornness which was the worst defect in his character.

"As long as I can draw down a hundred thousand dollars a fight, I'd be a fool to quit. I'm tougher than any of you think. A hundred thousand dollars!" His eyes gleamed with the old light. "The crowd roaring! And Iron Mike Brennon taking everything that's handed out, and finishing on his feet! No! No! I'll quit when I'm counted out-not before!"

"Mike!" the girl cried piercingly. "If you fight again, I'll swear I'll go away and never see you again!"

His gaze beat her eyes down, and her head sank on her breast. I never saw the human being-except one-who could stand the stare of Mike Brennon's magnetic eyes.

"Marjory," his deep voice vibrated with confidence, "you're just trying to bluff me into doing what you want me to do. But you're mine, and you always will be. You won't leave me, now. You can't!"

She hid her tear-blinded face in her hands and sobbed weakly. He stroked her bowed head tenderly. A failure in the ring perhaps, but outside of it Brennon had a power over those with whom he came in contact that none could overcome. The way he had beaten down the girl's weak pretense was almost brutal.

"Mike!" snarled Ganlon, speaking harshly and bitterly to hide his emotions; for a moment the hard-faced middleweight with his two hundred savage ring battles behind him, dominated the scene: "Mike, you're crazy! You got everything a man could want-things that most men work their lives out for and never get. You're on the borderline. You couldn't whip a second-rater.

"Costigan's as tough as you ever were. If I thought he'd flatten you with a punch or two, I'd say, go to it. But he won't. He'll knock you out, but it'll be after a smashin' that'll ruin you for life. You'll die, or you'll go to the bughouse. What good will your money, or Marjory's love do you then?"

Mike took his time about replying, and again his strange influence was felt like a cloud over the group.

"Costigan's over-rated. I'll show him up. He never saw the day he could take as much as I can, or hit as hard."

Spike made a despairing gesture, and turned away. Later he said to the girl and me: "No use arguin'. He thinks it's the money, but it ain't. The game's in his blood. And he's jealous of Mike Costigan. These iron men is terrible proud of their toughness. Remember how Van Heeren fought?"

"Win or lose, ten rounds with Costigan means Mike's finish. Each is too tough to be knocked out quick. It'll be a long, bloody grind, and it may finish Costigan, but it'll sure finish Mike. He'll end that fight dead, or punched nutty. At his best, Brennon would likely have wore Costigan down like he did Van Heeren. But Mike's gone away back, and Costigan is young-in his prime-which in a iron man is the same as sayin' you couldn't hurt him with a pile-driver."

MIKE BRENNON TRAINED conscientiously, as always. I discharged his sparring partners and had him punch the light bag for speed, and do a great deal of road work in a vain effort to recover some of the former steel spring quality of his weakening legs. But I knew it was useless. It was not a matter of conditioning-his trouble lay behind him in the thousands of cruel blows he had absorbed. A clever boxer may get out of condition, lose fights and come back; but when an iron man slips there is no comeback.

In the four months which preceded the Costigan fight, an air of gloom surrounded the camp which affected all but Mike himself. Marjory, after days of passionate pleading, sank into a sort of apathy. That he was being bitterly cruel to the girl never occurred to Mike, and we could not make him see it. He laughed at our fears as foolish, and insisted that he was practically in his prime. He swore that his fight with Slade, far from showing that he had slipped, proved that he was better than ever! For had he not beaten Slade, the most dangerous man in the ring? As for Costigan-a few rounds of savage slugging would send him down and out.

Mike was aware of his fistic faults; he frankly admitted that any second-rater who could avoid his swings could outpoint him; but he sincerely believed that he was still superior in ruggedness to any man that ever lived. And deep in his heart, I doubt if Mike really believed he would ever be knocked out.

One thing he insisted on; that Marjory should not see the fight. And she made one last plea for him to give it up.

"No use to start all that," he answered calmly. "Think, Marjory! My fourth hundred-thousand-dollar purse! That's a record few champions have set! One hundred thousand with Flash Sullivan-Gonzales-Slade- and now Costigan! Thousands of tickets sold in advance! I've got to go on now, anyhow. And I'm a cinch to win!"

CHAPTER VII. FRAMED.

AS IF IT were yesterday I visualize the scene; the ring bathed in the white glow above it; while the great crowd that filled the huge outside bowl swept away into the darkness of each side. A circle of white faces looked up from the ringside seats. Farther out only a twinkling army of glowing cigarettes evidenced the multitude, and a vast rippling undertone came from the soft darkness.

"Iron Mike Brennon, 190 pounds; in this corner, Iron Mike Costigan, 195!"

Brennon sat in his corner, head bowed, a contrast to the nervous, feline-like picture he had offered when he had paced the floor in his dressing-room. I wondered if he was still seeing the tear-stained face of Marjory as she kissed him in his dressing-room before he came into the ring.

When the men were called to the center of the ring for instructions, Mike, to my surprise, seemed apathetic. He walked with dragging feet. However, in front of his foe he came awake with fierce energy. Iron Mike Costigan was dark, with tousled black hair. Five feet eleven, and heavier than Brennon, what he lacked in lithe ranginess he made up in oak and iron massiveness.

The eyes of the two men burned into each other with savage intensity. Volcanic blue for Costigan; cold steel gray for

Brennon. Their sun-browned faces were set in unconscious snarls. But as they stood facing each other, Brennon's stare of concentrated cold ferocity wavered and fell momentarily before Costigan's savage blue eyes. I realized that this was the first man who had ever looked Mike down, and I thought of Corbett staring down Sullivan-of McGovern's eyes falling before Young Corbett's.

Then the men were back in their corners, and the seconds and handlers were climbing through the ropes. I hissed to Mike that I was going to throw in the sponge if the going got too rough, but he made no reply. He seemed to have sunk into that strange apathy again.

The gong!

Costigan hurtled from his corner, a compact bulk of fighting fury. Brennon came out more slowly. At my side Ganlon hissed: "What's the matter with Mike? He acts like he was drunk!"

The two Iron Mikes had met in the center of the ring. Costigan might have been slightly awed by the fame of the man he faced. At any rate he hesitated. Brennon walked toward his foe, but his feet dragged.

Then Costigan suddenly launched an attack, and shot a straight left to Brennon's face. As if the blow had roused him to his full tigerish fury, Mike went into action. The old sweeping haymakers began to thunder with all their ancient power. Costigan had, of course, no defense. A sweeping left-hander crashed under his heart with a sound like a caulking mallet striking a ship's side; a blasting right that whistled through the air, cannon-balled against his jaw. Costigan went down as though struck by a thunderbolt.

Then even as the crowd rose, he reeled up again. But I was watching Brennon. As though that sudden burst of action had taken all the strength out of him, he sagged against the ropes, limp, cloudy- eyed. Now sensing that his foe was up, he dragged himself forward with halting and uncertain motions.

Costigan, still dizzy from that terrific knockdown, was conscious of only one urge-the old instinct of the iron man-bore in and hit until somebody falls! Now he crashed through Brennon's groping arms and shot a right hook to the chin. Brennon swayed and fell, just as a drunken man falls when a prop against which he has been leaning is removed.

Over his motionless form the referee was counting: "Eight! Nine! Ten!" And the ring career of Iron Mike Brennon was at an end. A stunned silence reigned, and Iron Mike Costigan, new king of all iron men, leaned against the ropes, unable to believe his senses. Mike Brennon had been knocked out!

AROUND THE RING the typewriters of the reporters were ticking out the fall of a king: "Evidently Mike Brennon's famous iron jaw has at last turned to crockery after years of incredible bombardings...."

We carried Mike, still senseless, to his dressing-room. Ganlon was muttering under his breath, and as soon as we had Mike safe on a cot with a physician looking to him, the middleweight vanished. Marjory had been waiting for us and now she stood, white-faced and silent, by the cot where her lover lay.

At last he opened his eyes, and instantly he leaped erect, hands up. Then he halted, swayed and rubbed his eyes. Marjory was at his side in an instant and gently forced him back on the cot.

"What happened? Did I win?" he asked dazedly.

"You were knocked out in the first round, Mike." I felt it better to answer him directly. His eyes widened with amazement.

"I? Knocked out? Impossible!"

"Yes, Mike, you were," I assured him, expecting him to do any of the things I have seen fighters do on learning of their first knock- out-weep terribly, faint, rave and curse, or rush out looking for the conqueror. But being Mike Brennon and a never-to-be-solved enigma, he did none of these things. He merely rubbed his chin and laughed cynically.

"Guess I'd gone farther back than I thought. I don't remember the punch that put me out; funny thing-I've come through my last fight without a mark."

"And now you'll quit!" cried Marjory. "This is the best thing that could have happened to you. You promised you'd quit if you were knocked out, Mike." Her voice was painful in its intensity.

"Why, I wouldn't draw half a house now," Mike was beginning ruefully, when Ganlon burst in, eyes blazing.

"Mike!" he snarled. "Steve! Don't you two boneheads see there's somethin' wrong here? Mike, when did you begin feelin' drowsy?"

Brennon started. "That's right. I'd forgotten. I began feeling queer when I climbed in the ring. I sort of woke up when the referee was talking to us, and I remember how Costigan's eyes blazed. Then when I went back to my corner I got dizzy and drunken. Then I knew I was moving out in the ring and I saw Costigan through a fog. He hit me a hummer and I woke up and started swinging and saw him go down. That's the last I remember until I came to here."

Ganlon laughed bitterly. "Sure. You was out on your feet before Costigan hit you. A girl coulda pushed you over, and that's all Costigan done!"

"Doped!" I cried. "Costigan's crowd-or the gambling ring-"

"Naw-Mike's been crossed by the last person you'd think of. I been doin' some detective work. Mike, just before you left your dressin'-room, you drunk a small cup of tea, didn't you? Kinda unusual preparation for a hard fight, eh? But you drunk it to please somebody-"

Marjory was cowering in the corner. Mike was troubled and puzzled.

"But Spike, Marjory made that tea herself-"

"Yeah, and she doped it herself! She framed you to lose!"

OUR EYES TURNED on the shrinking girl-amazement in mine, anger in Ganlon's, and a deep hurt in Mike's.

"Marjory, why did you do that?" asked Mike, bewildered. "I might have won-"

"Yes, you might have won!" she cried in a sudden gust of desperate and despairing defiance. "After Costigan had battered you to a red ruin! Yes, I drugged the tea. It's my fault you were knocked out. You can't go back now, for you've lost your only attraction. You can't draw the crowds. I've gone through tortures since I first saw you lying on that cot after your fight with Slade-but you've only laughed at me. Now you'll have to quit. You're out of the game with a sound mind-that's all I care. I've saved you from your mad avarice and cruel pride in spite of yourself! And you can beat me now, or kill me-I don't care!"

For a moment she stood panting before us, her small fists clenched, then as no one spoke, all the fire went out of her. She wilted visibly and moved droopingly and forlornly toward the door. The wrap which enveloped her slender form, slid to the floor as she fumbled at the door-knob, revealing her in a cheap gingham dress. Mike, like a man awakening from a trance, started forward:

"Marjory! Where are you going? What are you doing in that rig?"

"It's the dress I was wearing when you first met me," she answered listlessly, "I wrote and got back my old job at the cafe."

He crossed the room with one stride, caught her slim shoulders and spun her around to face him, with unconsciously brutal force. "What do you mean?" he said.

She collapsed suddenly in a storm of weeping. "Don't you hate me for drugging you?" she sobbed. "I didn't think you'd ever want to see me again."

He crushed her to him hungrily. "Girl, I swear I didn't realize how it was hurting you. I thought you were foolish-willful. I couldn't see how you were suffering. But you've opened my eyes. I must have been insane! You're right-it was pride-senseless vanity-I couldn't see it then, but I do now. I didn't understand that I was ruining your happiness. And that's all that matters now, dear. We've got our life and love before us, and if it rests with me, you're going to be happy all the rest of your life."

Ganlon beckoned me and I followed him out. For the only time since I had known him, Mike's hard face had softened. The sentiment that lies at the base of the Irish nature, however deeply hidden sometimes, made his steely eyes almost tender.

"I had her down all wrong," Ganlon said softly. "I take back everything I might have said about her. She's a regular- and Mike- well, he's the only iron man I ever knew that got the right breaks at last."

THE END

www.ingramcontent.com/pod-product-compliance
Lightning Source LLC
Chambersburg PA
CBHW020919180626
46816CB00007BA/2475